This book is for Henry and Eve,
who are actually quite
well behaved. It's just
that their father is nuts.

SIMON & SCHUSTER BOOKS FOR YOUNG READERS

An imprint of Simon & Schuster Children's Publishing Division

1230 Avenue of the Americas, New York, New York 10020

SIMON & SCHUSTER BOOKS FOR YOUNG READERS is a trademark of Simon & Schuster, Inc.

For information about special discounts for bulk purchases, please contact Simon & Schuster Special

Sales at 1-866-506-1949 or business@simonandschuster.com.

The Simon & Schuster Speakers Bureau can bring authors to your live event. For more information or

to book an event, contact the Simon & Schuster Speakers Bureau at 1-866-248-3049 or visit our website

at www.simonspeakers.com.

Book design by Lucy Ruth Cummins

The text for this book is set in Grit Primer.

The illustrations for this book are rendered in ink and watercolor.

Manufactured in China

0314 SCP

2 4 6 8 10 9 7 5 3 1

Library of Congress Cataloging-in-Publication Data

Kaplan, Bruce Eric, author, illustrator.

Meaniehead / Bruce Eric Kaplan. — First edition.

pages cm

Summary: Henry and Eve are going through a phase of fighting with each other all the time,

and their battle quickly escalates from arguing over a toy to leaving a path of destruction

across the United States and beyond.

ISBN 978-1-4424-8542-6 (hardcover : alk. paper) — ISBN 978-1-4424-8543-3 (ebook)

[1. Brothers and sisters—Fiction. 2. Behavior—Fiction. 3. Tall tales] I. Title.

PZ7.K128973Me 2014

[E]—dc23

2013016385

MEANIEHEAD

BRUCE ERIC KAPLAN

Simon & Schuster Books for Young Readers

New York   London   Toronto   Sydney   New Delhi

Henry and Eve were going through a new, terrible phase of fighting with each other all the time.

One day they both reached for the same action

figure at the exact same time.

"Meaniehead!" Eve screamed.

"It's mine!" Henry screamed back at her.

There's nothing sillier than fighting about what belongs to whom, but no kids and even fewer adults know that.

Because of all the fuss,

their mother's favorite lamp broke.

Both blamed the other person.

One thing led to another, and somehow Henry

wrecked Eve's bedroom,

plus the rest of the neighborhood.

All that was left of Eve's doll collection was just

one dirty little doll head which smelled of smoke.

"Look what you did!" she screamed, and raced

after him, but he was too fast for her.

Luckily, she found a bulldozer.

As she chased after Henry, Eve

drove down Main Street and bulldozed their favorite toy store,

then the library,

then the pizza place,

then the beauty parlor,

then every other building in town,

plus the park.

Their town was now completely demolished.

Henry and Eve stopped and

had a snack.

Then they started fighting again.

They made their way down to

San Diego, where they caused a big ruckus at the zoo and all the animals got loose.

They made their way across the country, causing destruction wherever they went.

They really liked the Grand Canyon

but their squabbling created an avalanche

which totally flattened it.

In Texas they met up with two very aggressive

football teams, who took sides, and

they all ended up demolishing the entire state.

And very quickly after that they moved through the rest of the country and destroyed it.

So they chased each other onto a plane that went to Hawaii.

Shortly thereafter, Henry and Eve caused every volcano there to explode.

Which in turn caused the world to blow up.

So now the world was gone.

And Henry and Eve floated in space far, far away

from each other.

Henry was sad.

He didn't want to fight with Eve anymore.

Eve felt the same way.

And somehow, miraculously, they found their way

back to each other.

They laughed about what a crazy fight they had had

and both vowed never to destroy the world again.